For Jeannie Veltz—from your biggest fans, Beth and Osbert
E. C. K.

For Audrey and Flynn—Don't lend out the family helicopter to penguins
or you will be picking dried seaweed snacks out of the seats for weeks.
H. B. L.

First edition 2009

Library of Congress Cataloging-in-Publication Data
Kimmel, Elizabeth Cody.
My penguin Osbert in love / Elizabeth Cody Kimmel ;
illustrated by H. B. "Buck" Lewis. —1st ed
p. cm.
Summary: When Osbert the penguin shows up on his doorstep
with several friends and an invitation to Aurora Australis'
party at the South Pole, Joe decides to transport them there in the
helicopter he received this year for Christmas.
ISBN 978-0-7636-3032-4
[1. Penguins—Fiction. 2. Helicopters—Fiction. 3. Friendship—Fiction. 4. South Pole—Fiction.]
I. Lewis, H. B., ill. II. Title.
PZ7.K56475Os 2008
[E]—dc22   2007052888

2 4 6 8 10 9 7 5 3 1

Printed in China

This book was typeset in Colwell.
The illustrations were done in watercolor, pastel, and digital rendering.

Candlewick Press
99 Dover Street
Somerville, Massachusetts 02144

visit us at www.candlewick.com

My Penguin
Osbert in Love

Elizabeth Cody Kimmel

illustrated by

H. B. "Buck" Lewis

CANDLEWICK PRESS

I had just put away my new helicopter and was cleaning out my ant farm when I heard a knock.

I thought it might be the mailman with my package—I had ordered a new wing for the ant farm. So I ran downstairs and opened the door.

Right in the middle of the welcome mat, I saw a familiar face. It was my penguin, Osbert! Santa gave me Osbert for Christmas last year, and Osbert had been living at the zoo.

Apparently, Osbert had brought along a few friends.

I wanted to ask them all in, but I didn't want my mom to see them. She might not be so happy that Osbert had staged a zoo break. Plus, she worries a lot about her carpets. So we snuck upstairs to my room.

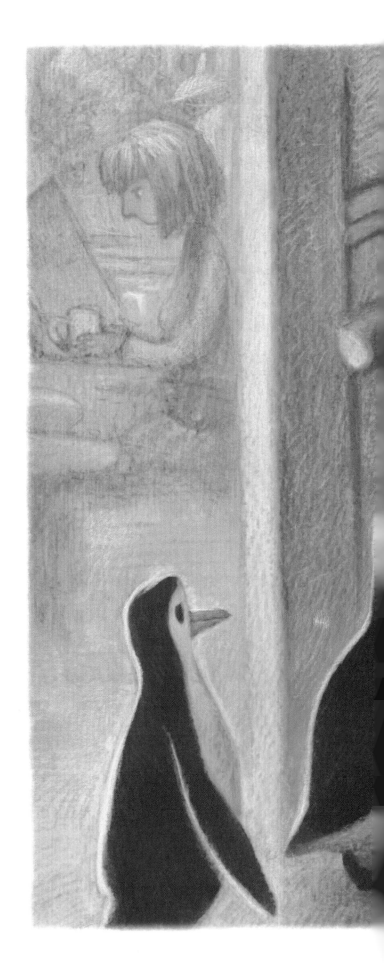

Osbert had an invitation tucked under his wing. When I opened it up, all the penguins gathered around and sighed.

ONCE-IN-A-CENTURY SOUTH POLE EXTRAVAGANZA!

Please join us on February 14 for the centennial gathering to witness the southern lights! Be there with your friends as Antarctica's sky explodes in a dazzling display that only Mother Nature can provide.

Yours sincerely,

Aurora Australis

AURORA AUSTRALIS
PRESIDENT
PENGUIN LIFE SOCIETY
SOUTH POLE

BLACK TIE REQUESTED   NO RSVP NECESSARY

When I put the invitation down, twenty-two pairs of penguin eyes were watching me.

My relatives were coming in from all over the country that day for my mom's Midwinter Bash. I had to be there. But Osbert wanted me to help him get to the South Pole. And Osbert was my friend.

We checked the globe. From my house to Antarctica, it looked like a pretty straight shot due south.

Now, everyone knows penguins can't fly.

But I can. This year, Santa gave
me my very own helicopter!

I left my mom a note:

Mom,
I'm taking the helicopter out for a little spin.
Don't worry—I packed my warm red sweater.

Love,
Joe

P.S. I promise I will not be late for the Bash.

I had a little trouble getting everybody into their seat belts, but we managed to take off before noon.

We'd been flying south for a really long time when Osbert nudged me with his wing. I picked a quiet-looking spot and landed the helicopter. When we'd all gotten out, a man in a flowered shirt came over and offered us drinks. Apparently, we had not flown far enough south.

It was way past lunchtime, and the penguins were taking a bathroom break. I didn't know how we'd ever get there in time.

But Osbert was my friend. And he wanted me to help him get to the South Pole.

We'd been flying south for a really, *really* long time when Osbert poked me with his beak. I looked down and saw snow-capped mountains. I found a nice flat spot and landed the helicopter. When we'd all gotten out, a little girl selling T-shirts came over to us.

Apparently, we had still not flown far enough south.

Everyone was really friendly, but it was getting dark, and in my wildest dreams I couldn't imagine how we were ever going to get there in time.

But Osbert was my friend. Osbert couldn't fly. And he wanted me to help him get to the South Pole.

We'd been flying south for a really, really, *really* long time when Osbert prodded me with his foot. I looked down. At first I thought we were flying through a giant cloud. But then I realized it was snow— snow everywhere.

The South Pole.

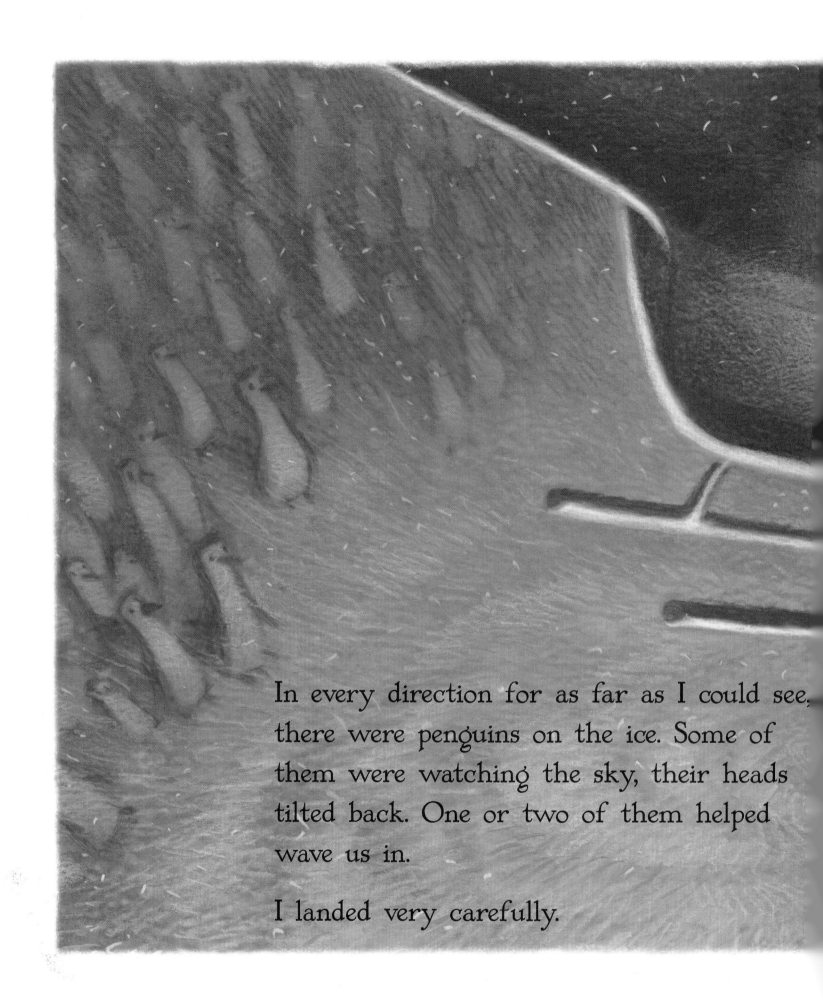

In every direction for as far as I could see, there were penguins on the ice. Some of them were watching the sky, their heads tilted back. One or two of them helped wave us in.

I landed very carefully.

Fortunately, Osbert and the penguins were already wearing their party clothes. I put on a black tie over my warm red sweater, and we all jumped out.

Wow! The southern lights were even better than the invitation had said. We didn't have anything like this back home! It was way better than any sunset or fireworks show.

But when I turned to tell Osbert how great it was, he wasn't looking at the lights.

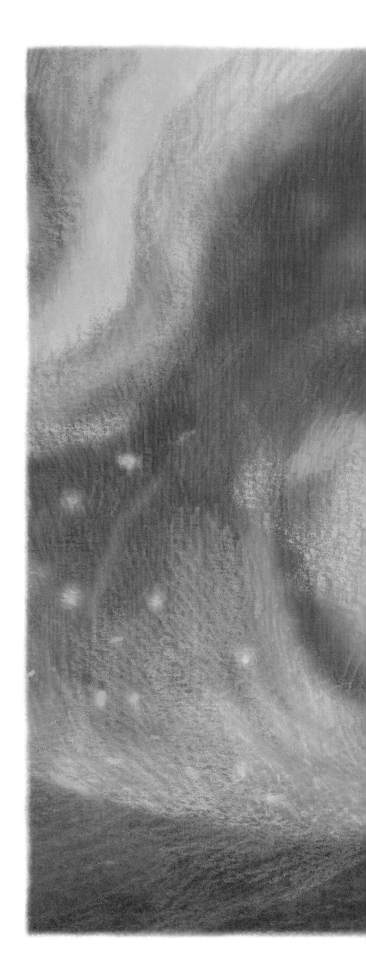

Osbert was staring at a penguin who had waddled out of the crowd. It was Aurora Australis. Osbert's beak dropped open a little, and his eyes got huge. He wiggled his flippers and sucked in his stomach.

Osbert was my friend. Osbert couldn't fly. He had wanted me to help him get to the South Pole, and I had done it. But Osbert didn't want to look at the southern lights now. He was looking at Aurora Australis. And she looked back at him. They stared into each other's penguin eyes.

Osbert was in love.

My toes were getting cold, and my stomach was starting to growl. I was ready to head home. But before I could say anything, Osbert and Aurora started a game of flipperball.

I waited patiently, but a little icicle started to form on my black tie.

When Aurora started to bellyslide on an iceberg, Osbert jumped right in to race her. When they couldn't decide who had won, Osbert suggested a do-over.

I reminded Osbert
that I had to be home in
time for my mom's party, but he
gave me the "just a minute" flipper. He
and Aurora started making a giant snow
penguin. Meanwhile, another icicle formed
right next to the first one. And my red
sweater had frozen stiff. I knew that if I
didn't leave right away, I would be late for
the Midwinter Bash.

As if all this weren't bad enough, I realized I needed a bathroom break. Back on the ice, Osbert and Aurora were making a second snow penguin to keep the first one company. I called out to Osbert, but he didn't even hear me. I had to find my way to the Polar Restroom Facilities all alone, in the dark.

I walked back to the helicopter, hanging my head. Now it was snowing, and I couldn't see Osbert anywhere. But Osbert was Aurora's friend now, and I had to go. There was no time for a final good-bye.

I tried to get into the helicopter, but there was something in my way.

The helicopter was full of penguins, including Osbert and Aurora! I threw my arms around Osbert. Aurora patted my head with her flipper, so I gave her a little hug, too. She smelled like seaweed, but in a nice way.

I asked Osbert if he was absolutely sure they wanted to come back north with me. He nodded, and all the other penguins did, too.

To be honest, I'm not exactly sure that the other penguins in the helicopter were the same ones we'd started with. But Osbert was definitely the same old Osbert.

Osbert and Aurora were both my friends. They were both coming, and I was going to fly us all home. With any luck, we'd even make it to the Midwinter Bash.

On the last leg of the trip, I let Osbert take the controls.

It turns out, penguins can fly really well.

THROW YOUR OWN MIDWINTER BASH!

Invite your friends over for a party that will light up a dark winter afternoon and chase the stuck-in-the-zoo blues away. Using multicolored markers, construction paper, and a little glitter and glue, you can easily make your own beautiful southern lights invitations. Ask your friends to come in costume. All you need to dress up like Osbert or Aurora is a white T-shirt and a hooded sweatshirt! But since it's a party, how about throwing on a bow tie? If you're really stuck, just wear a red sweater like Joe.

As for penguin treats, we all know that Osbert prefers cold creamed herring and seaweed jam. Your guests might prefer Joe's favorite chocolate chip waffles, though. Or you could ask an adult to help you prepare these special South Pole snacks:

Southern Lights Extravaganza Punch

INGREDIENTS:

1/2 gallon rainbow sherbet
2 quarts ginger ale
1 cup cranberry juice

DIRECTIONS:

Empty entire container of rainbow sherbet into a punch bowl. (Allow sherbet to soften slightly beforehand so that it can be easily removed from the container.) Pour ginger ale and cranberry juice over the top and watch the colors swirl into the punch. Using a large toothpick, tape, and a small strip of paper, make a flag that says SOUTH POLE and stick it into your sherbet iceberg.

Black-and-White Penguin Cookies

INGREDIENTS:

1 cup unsalted butter
1 3/4 cups white sugar
4 eggs
1 cup milk
1 teaspoon vanilla extract
1/2 teaspoon lemon extract
2 1/2 cups cake flour
2 1/2 cups all-purpose flour
1 teaspoon baking powder
1/2 teaspoon salt
4 cups confectioners' sugar
1/3 cup boiling water
8 oz. square semi-sweet chocolate, chopped

DIRECTIONS:

1. Preheat oven to 375° F (190° C). Grease 2 baking sheets.

2. Mix together butter and sugar in a bowl until smooth. Beat in eggs one at a time, then stir in the milk, vanilla, and lemon extract. In a separate bowl, combine cake flour, all-purpose flour, baking powder, and salt; gradually blend into the creamed mixture. Using a 1/4 cup measure scoop, drop the dough spaced about 2 inches apart on baking sheets.

3. Bake until edges begin to brown, about 20 to 30 minutes. Transfer to a wire rack and allow to cool completely.

4. To make frosting, place confectioners' sugar in a large bowl. Mix in boiling water one tablespoon at a time until mixture is thick and spreadable. (Add more than the indicated amount if you need to.)

5. Transfer half of the frosting to the top of a double boiler set over simmering water. Stir in the chocolate. Warm the mixture, stirring frequently, until the chocolate melts. Remove from heat.

6. With a brush, coat half of each cookie with chocolate frosting and the other half with the white frosting. Set on waxed paper until frosting hardens.